# The Taste of Rain

## Further recent titles from LinguaBooks

**Theatre**
Narrowboat Blues
Puss in Boots
Aladdin

**Fantasy**
The Legend of Sidora

**Fiction**
A Parting Shot

**Language**
Gateway English


More information from
www.linguabooks.com

# The Taste of Rain

### and other stories

## A miscellany of modern fiction

LinguaBooks

The right of the individual authors to be identified as the authors of the stories included in this collection has been asserted in accordance with sections 77 and 78 of the Copyright, Designs and Patents Act 1988.

ISBN (paperback edition): 978-1911369578
eISBN (digital edition): 978-1911369585

First edition
Editor: Ann Claypole
Copyright © 2022 LinguaBooks

A CIP catalogue record for this book is available from the British Library.

LinguaBooks
Elsie Whiteley Innovation Centre
Hopwood Lane. Halifax HX1 5ER
United Kingdom
www.linguabooks.com

*Stories are medicine. They have such power; they do not require that we do, be, act anything – we need only listen.*

– Clarissa Pinkola Estes

# Contents

# Introduction

These stories span many decades and celebrate a diversity of authors, nationalities and locations.

There is no single unifying characteristic to these tales; rather, they are inhabited by characters who are at times naturalistic and at others an embodiment of the imaginary world they inhabit. From the mystical elements of the title story to the mythical dancers in Ghostly Laughter and the quirky characters of Dotty and Blacky, the authors of these stories draw the reader into a world of shifting realities, questioning relationships and morally diverse individuals inhabiting a whole range of worlds from the mundane to the fantastic.

The key to gripping fiction is a keen observation of human nature, not always manifested in broad, sweeping landscapes of emotion, but often in the minutiae of human life and spaces in between our existence. Above all, these stories offer variety, pathos and contemplation combined with an occasional surprise and a touch of humour.

But above all, these are tales about people real and imagined, their virtues and their foibles and the lessons to be learned from their attempts to come to grips with the human condition.

# The Taste of Rain

by Maurice Claypole

## The Taste of Rain

# 1

His body darted forward as the sickening crunch filled his ears, the shock of both sensations almost instantly buffered by the whoosh of the twin airbags. "What the…!"

Cal flung open the door to the darkness outside, but already the driver of the car in front was in his face, shouting abuse through the pouring rain and flashing lights. Had he lost concentration? Dozed for a moment, skidded on the wet surface? His brain couldn't quite get it together; in the passenger seat, Cassie was screaming in panic but clearly unhurt, thank God. Eventually, the other motorist calmed down, the drivers exchanged insurance details and Cal slumped back into the driver's seat.

Still in shock, he turned to check on Cassie, but she was no longer in the car. He could just make out her shape flickering in and out of existence at the side of the road, repeatedly picked out and then discarded by the headlights of passing cars. What Cal couldn't understand was that her head seemed to be tilted back as the rain beat down on her face.

"I still don't know what happened," Cal started, "I remember seeing his brake lights and then..."

"Doesn't matter," soothed Cassie, blissfully calm. "Nobody was hurt, and the insurance takes care of everything else."

"Yes, but..."

"Shhhh... it's nearly over, but everything will be all right."

Not sure what she meant, Cal did what he always did at moments like this. He kept his peace.

## 2

With hindsight, that was probably the first time he had realised that there was something odd, something otherworldly, about Cassie. And it was the first time he had actually seen her do it. The second time was on holiday on the Mediterranean island of Malta. After a couple of lazy days at Mellieha Bay, they had caught the bus to St. Julian's just as the sun was going down. Cal was up for a bit of nightlife, hanging out and smoking shisha in the street cafes of Paceville, but Cassie seemed tired and edgy and keen to head back to the peace and quiet of their little hotel.

As a result, they ended up having a silly, pointless little argument, the kind of thing that in earlier years might have been called a lover's tiff, and Cassie had run off toward the beach with Cal in slow pursuit. When he eventually caught her up, the skies had darkened and a warm rain was falling earthwards, borne gently on a sea breeze – and there she was, adopting that same pose he had vaguely witnessed in the darkness, her head tilted full back and this time, he could see not only that her arms were outstretched as though in worship, but that her mouth was wide open and her tongue extended, savouring the rain.

At first she refused to talk about it – no, refuse is the wrong word; that would imply conflict, a defence mechanism or a sense of hostility that was simply not present. Throughout the rest of the holiday, she merely declined to explain, but at that moment, as she lowered her head and turned to him, no explanation was necessary, for the warmth and joy reflected in her expression and the renewed sparkle in her eyes quelled any antagonism he might have felt and set the tone for the rest of their stay on the island as they enjoyed both the local nightlife and the pleasure of one another's company in the quieter moments.

## 3

Cassie had always known. And yet, as she reclined on the scanner table, her knees bent and supported by a large piece of foam plastic, she still dreaded what the MRI scan would reveal. They had given her earplugs to protect against the deafening whirring and clanking of the powerful magnets as this wonder of modern technology set about its ominous task. When it was over and she had dressed and reclaimed her keys, watch and wedding ring from the locker, Cal was waiting to take her home. Dependable, loving Cal; he would have to know, he deserved to know. He deserved the gift.

## 4

Champagne glasses clinked, bodies swayed lithely to the rumba, meeting hearts beat in unison, then raced faster and faster, finally relaxing, serene and joyful.

"Happy anniversary, darling."

"Happy anniversary, Cal," then a pause. "There's something I have to tell you, something I need to tell you. I just want you to understand that I can't tell you yet."

"So you're telling me that there's something you have to tell me, but can't tell me? Is it to do with your test results?"

"No, yes; partly. But you don't have to worry; everything will be all right."

"You said that once before, when…"

"I know. That's why we have to wait."

"Wait? Why? For what?"

"We have to wait for the rain. Remember when we lost the baby? It helped me get through a terrible time – and soon it will help you. This is going to sound weird, but…"

Cal put his hand on her arm, gently interrupting her flow.

"I think I know what you're going to say. I've seen you do it. I've seen you drink the rain."

"Yes, but it has to be the right sort of rain. The right moment."

"But how do you know?"

"When you have tasted it just once, you know."

Faintly, as though from a distance, came a gentle susurration – not the pitter-patter of a children's rhyme, but a continuous whispering of fine spray against the walls and windows, an enchanting shushing sound that seemed to say, "hush, hush, I am here for you."

As Cassie handed him the letter from the clinic, the panic came over him in waves, stabbing him in the chest. He knew what the letter contained. He could hardly breathe. The swishing sound outside grew fiercer, louder, its attraction stronger.

"I spoke to the doctor,' she said, 'we don't have much time."

He was gasping for breath. He had feared the worst but been unable to believe it. He was going to lose her. The foreboding denial was replaced by deadly certainty as he stood transfixed, incapable of speech. Cassie took him by the hand and led him gently out onto the porch, where he remained as if in a stupor, watching her step into the spuming cascade, tilt her head back and drink in the nectar of the gods.

After a moment, she returned to him, put her arms around him, seemingly breaking the spell. He drew her to him and as they kissed, his panic subsided. Intoxicated by the taste of the rain on her lips, he savoured the moment. In the midst of his anguish, something magical was happening. He felt calmer, stronger, ready to face the dark days ahead.

"That's what it all means," he began, "Now I can…"

"Yes," she whispered. "Now you can taste the rain. I told you everything will be all right. It is my gift to you. I don't need it any more."

# Tea for Two

by Anthony Curtis

## Tea for Two

I hesitated before ringing the doorbell and flinched when I heard the trembling voice.

"Who is it?"

"My name is Matthews, Mrs Brent. I moved in yesterday. I have the flat opposite you."

"What do you want?"

"I'm afraid I've run out of sugar."

"Oh dear, it's rather difficult. Never mind. Just a moment, please."

I waited. After a while, a bolt was drawn and a key turned. The door opened. She stood framed in the doorway, epitomising all the sweet old ladies that have ever lived. And I wanted to run.

"You'd better come in, Mr... er..." "Matthews."

"Oh, yes. I'm afraid I've dropped the sugar. I'm blind, you see."

How glad I was she could not see my face.

Tea for Two

"I'm terribly sorry," I said as I entered the room. "May I put the light on?"

"Oh, how silly of me; I forget, you know. The switch is on the left, close to the door."

I switched the light on. I glanced at the living room as we passed through it to the kitchen. I had expected aspidistras and chiffon lace, but was confronted with polished chrome, sheer white and, apart from a pair of pale yellow curtains, a distinct lack of colour.

"May I offer you some tea?" she asked when I had swept up the sugar from the tiled floor. "I do hope you won't feel that I'm being forward, but I seldom have visitors."

I wanted to say no, but couldn't. Months before, when she had been able to see, I had watched her from my window across the street as she tended her plants on the balcony.

In the following months, we often took tea together. We spoke of many things, but she never mentioned the cause of her blindness, and I dared not.

I was struck by her stoicism, by her laughter, which defied her dark loneliness, and when I visited her, she always greeted me

21

with "How nice to see you." To see me!

I told her I was a struggling writer, and she playfully suggested I was using her as a character study. I laughed with her, of course, but inwardly, my soul cried in anguish. I realise now that man is primarily self-centred, that in the final analysis, he thinks only of himself.

Then one bright evening in the summer, in chrome-reflected and white-absorbed sunlight, we met for the last time. I distinctly remember the stain on the tablecloth as I upset my tea.

"You've never learned to live with it, have you?" she said.

"With what?" I spluttered.

She felt for my arm and laid her hand on it.

"Please don't make it harder, young man. Remember the first time you came to see me? You addressed me as Mrs Brent. That was a mistake, my dear. Not long after my accident, my husband passed away and I reverted to my maiden name. I instructed the caretaker to change the name-plate downstairs. How you knew my married name has puzzled me ever since. And you never inquired as to the cause of my blindness. I thought at first that you did not want to be inquisitive, but now I know."

Her fingers grasped my arm in a vice-like grip.

"Why?" she asked. "Why did you come? Has your conscience been pricking you all this time?"

I sat there staring at her unseeing eyes, wishing that I had a stone to crawl under.

"Shall I tell you how often in the last months I have thought of revenge?" People say that it is sweet, but the thought is actually sour. One thing I've learned, however, is that you are suffering more than I am. I've learned to live with my blindness. Can you live with your guilt? Perhaps it will ease your conscience when I tell you that there is a good chance that I will regain my eyesight. The operation is expensive, but I can afford it."

She must have felt the renewed tension in my arm, for she said, "No, I require no further help from you. All those anonymous payments into my account. I wonder how you obtained the number."

Much to my relief she let go of my arm.

The sun had gone and the room was in semi-darkness. I went to the door and switched on the light. I sat down again and she said, "You were drunk that night, weren't you? I'd often read of hit-and-run drivers in the newspapers, but never dreamed of being one of their victims."

Tears streamed down my cheeks. "Please don't," I sobbed.

She laid her hand once more on my arm and began to stroke it.

"Hush," she said softly. "It's over now, no more sleepless nights."

She stood up, her expression hardening as she said, "You'd better go now; it's been a trying experience for us both."

"Will I ever see you again?" I croaked. For God help me, I loved her.

She shrugged. "It's strange, but I can't say yes and I can't say no. It's really up to you, I suppose."

As I went out of the door, I thought I heard her say, "You needn't turn off the light."

# The Killer in Me

by Jean Meyer Brandenberg

# The Killer in Me

I ran in through the back door, throwing the axe down as I entered. The fly-door slammed behind me. I rushed into the bathroom and kicked off my shoes. The lino was cold. I turned on the shower and hoped that the embers in the old stove had kept the water tank warm. I took off my green blouse; blood was spattered all over the front, and it had gone onto my skirt. I felt the blood on my face, it was still warm. I stepped over the edge of the old, white-enamelled iron bath and stood under the shower. The water was reasonably hot. I started to wash the blood out of my hair and off my face. I had to get rid of the evidence. I hadn't killed before. There had to be a first time.

I didn't want anyone to find me like this. I leaned out of the bath, picked up my blouse and skirt and started to feverishly wash out the blood before it stained. Coming to the country like this was certainly not a good idea. Nor was renting this old place. It was cheap, that's true, but it was also a school for killing – a murder scene.

Blood was on my hands. How could I get away from here? My car radiator had boiled dry. I was virtually a prisoner in my own backyard. But I had to get away. I heard noises, the sound of the front door opening and footsteps. "Joan, are you there?" I heard a man's voice call out. I remembered I had invited my friend Dan to come down and visit from the city. I had promised him dinner. I heard him come in. "What on earth is this?" he exclaimed. He walked down the passage, the fly-door opened and shut twice as he went out and came in again. I knew he had seen the blood spots on the lino and the body out in the yard. The game is up, I thought. Better that I confessed to him than to anyone else. I wrapped a towel around me and opened the door. I hoped that there was no more blood on me.

Dan stared at me with a grim look on his face. "Don't you know how to kill a chook properly?" he asked, breaking into a smile.

# The Scarlet Dress

by Arja Faller-Nenonen

## The Scarlet Dress

My mother ran a small but exclusive dressmaking business. I could sit in the waiting room doing my homework or flicking through the latest Paris fashion magazines for hours, observing the comings and goings of the customers at the same time. My favourite fashions were the bridal and evening dresses, which I studied and copied for the princesses I liked to draw. They were far more glamorous and beautiful than any of my mother's customers, who were often wealthy, but disappointingly for me, neither young and glamorous nor beautiful.

When my mother told me that there was a dress to be delivered, I was always very keen to go anywhere. I was a curious child. I loved being sent to posh houses to deliver dresses. Most customers liked to collect theirs in person in order to try them on before they paid and took them away. But there were a few even more exclusive clients who totally trusted my mother and wanted their dresses delivered. One of these was a small round lady, the wife of a famous portrait artist called Alfred Alopeus. She always presented my mother with the most amazing new fabrics, which was very unusual in 1949, when most mortals were lucky to have any fabric at all for a new dress. Very often a customer would bring two old dresses which were carefully picked apart and, under my mother's clever design skills, transformed into one fashionable dress. Mrs Alopeus' fabrics were different – exotic fabrics in brilliant colours. For me, it was like watching a magician pull a white rabbit out of a hat when Mrs Alopeus came and opened her bag and pulled out another fantastic silk, causing a lot of oohs and aahs from the 'girls'. Mother told us that the lady's nephew was the Finnish ambassador to Peking, which was supposed to explain it all.

This time the fabric was of brilliant red satin. The dress was deeply décolleté with enormous puff sleeves and a very wide long skirt, which had eaten up miles of fabric. It was carefully packed in a cardboard box with tissue paper between the folds. The Alopeuses lived in a part of town which had been spared the air raids. It was called Eira, which reminded me of the opera. My mother was an opera fan, and I knew of a famous Finnish singer, Maria Eira, who seldom appeared in her native country. Eira is still one of the poshest parts of Helsinki, crammed with houses built in the Finnish National Romantic style. They were made of huge grey or red granite blocks and carved with fantastic ornaments. I loved having an excuse to go there. It was a long tram journey, and I held the box with the scarlet satin dress in my arms as if it were a baby. My arms ached. This was an important mission for me, and I had to come home with money in my pocket.

There before me was a huge grey-granite edifice with a turret. I checked and double checked the address. The place looked like a palace. I would have liked to be a princess shut up in there. I was twelve and a hopeless romantic, drawing castles on steep mountains with princes and princesses. Now I was about to enter one of my dream castles.

I watched the house for an eternity before I rang the bell. A maid opened the door.

"I have a dress to deliver," I whispered in a

conspiratorial fashion.

"Oh yes, I know. Just wait a moment," the maid said and left me standing in a huge entrance hall with parquet floor and Persian carpets.

An enormous chandelier hung from the ceiling and up on one wall was a full-length portrait of a beautiful young lady wearing the same dress that I was delivering.

I said to myself, "It really is the same dress, the same fabric, the same style, the same model."

But the lady in the portrait was young and slim and beautiful. She looked like a younger version of Mrs Alopeus. Could it be her daughter? Just at that moment, an elderly man appeared. He had a goatee beard, long grey hair and spectacles. He wore grey tweeds, such as I always imagined Englishmen to wear when hunting.

He said, with a slight foreign accent, "I see you admire the portrait of my wife. She is very beautiful. I do not need any other models."

This puzzled me more. Either my eyes were playing tricks on me, or I was dreaming. The old man did not even look at the dress and I did not see Mrs Alopeus at all. I handed him the dress box and presented the bill. I was paid and given a handsome tip.

Before I could open my mouth to form a question, I was out in the street again. I didn't take the tram but walked all the way home thinking about the portrait and the dress. Mother wondered where on earth I had been. She had been worried about me but was glad I was home safe with the money. When I told her about the portrait, she laughed and said I had imagined it all, and that I had read too many fairy tales.

We never saw Mrs Alopeus again, nor heard anything of her artist husband, but the image of that portrait remains forever imprinted on my memory.

# The Farmer's Son

by Anthony Curtis

# The Farmer's Son

I met him at a farm. He didn't need to chew a straw; his bleary, bulging eyes that never seemed to be able to focus on any particular point, his idiot grin and his red, weather-beaten face, which he never seemed to have washed, told their own story.

And everybody loved him.

His secret, if he ever had one, was that he loved everybody and everything. He just couldn't think 'bad thinks' (his own words).

One day he told me that he had only one enemy in the world, and that was himself. I was the second, but he never knew it.

The girls laughed at him, and he drooled at the girls, and I believe that if an atom bomb had exploded under his feet, he would have emerged from the catastrophe grinning broadly, saying that the world was just having its little joke.

His parents adored him. They told me that he had never been sick in his life, that he walked in the footsteps of saints, and that he would live for ever.

He worked on his parents' farm, which was ninety percent horses and ten percent chickens. His job was to feed the horses, so he was occupied for most of the day.

I had no choice but to lodge at the farm, for it was the only cheap accommodation available in those parts. My boss at the office was too stingy to allow me an expense account, so every evening I ate with the family at the farm. This meant sitting opposite him as he shovelled home-cooked food into his foolish face.

More than once, I asked myself, "He's just a country bumpkin. Why should I bother with him at all?"

I knew the answer, of course. He was better than I was. Thinking of all the petty crimes I had committed in my life. I knew I was not worthy to step into his muddy boots.

"What is it that makes you so ugly?" I asked him once – rather cruelly, I must admit.

"Ugliness is in the eye of the beholder," was his answer, and I turned my back on him and quickly walked away, for I realised with a shock that I had met my match – in a country bumpkin.

In retrospect, I think it's quite likely that I would eventually have done him in, for I hated his smugness, but as it happened, someone, or rather something, did the job for me.

One evening I came back from the office, and he wasn't there.

"'E's in the 'ospital," said the father. "A 'orse bit 'e," said the mother.

"Why aren't you with him, then?" I asked.

"Don't you worry none, 'e ain't gonna die," said the father.

I found out the name of the hospital and drove there without a moment's hesitation, breaking the speed limit all the way.

The horse had bitten him in the neck.

"You said you never think bad thinks," I said. "What about the horse? He bit you didn't he? You must be thinking bad thinks about him."

"No," said the bumpkin, and I had to lean over to catch his words.

"You've got it orl wrong. If the horse 'ad 'ated me, he would've kicked me to death. It was a love bite. 'E didn't know 'is own strength..."

And with those words he ascended into heaven.

My boss at the office has a new assistant now. The old couple feed the ten percent chickens. I feed the ninety percent horses. In the evenings, I sit at the supper table and eat in silence, while the mother and father finger their rosaries and pray for the return of their son.

# Coastal Encounter

by Shelly Bowers

## Coastal Encounter

Every time I close my eyes and all I can see is a lonely old woman looking at me. The image of all my fears in life, she stands alone on the grey coastal road, alone in the wind and the rain, alone in her dreams and visions. I wish I had known her name, but now I don't even know if she was real. Yet I can still feel the pain of her story. It frightened me to see and touch the sorrow and loneliness that can cripple a mortal mind and shadow the human heart.

As for myself, I had just broken off my long-term relationship with John and, needing a holiday, I picked a cycling break around Ireland to help me 'discover myself', as the cliché goes. The weather had been dull all morning, threatening gales, so struggling to balance a bike and put on waterproofs, I tried to push ahead out of Cushendall. Walking along the road towards me was an elderly lady, heading into town. She smiled as we came to pass and I knew we were about to have a five minute conversation on the weather. It is an art perfected in Ireland. I tried to push the bike forward eager to reach the youth hostel, but I was too late and with a forced grin, I responded to an ambiguous comment about the miserable state of the sky. We stood together on the road and exchanged pleasantries on my holiday. Then, like a bolt from the blue, she changed the subject to ask me what kind of men I liked.

"You know, attracted to," she prompted.

I must have stood with my mouth open. This was a subject that I had rarely discussed with my mother without thinking of having a discussion with my grandmother, whom I judged to be a good ten years younger than this lady.

To me this scene had suddenly become so comical. My heart warmed to her youthful ways, as I stammered out that I was attracted to tall blond men.

"Ah! So you like the Scandinavian types with their big muscles," she laughed, nudging me in a conspiratorial manner, "I like dark swarthy men, with dark eyes which capture your soul."

Her voice became wistful against the wind and the waves.

"So it's an Italian you are after," I joked.

"No! No!" she said, "I like the men from the East, the desert places. You know, the Gulf and Kuwait."

The story she then told me was typical of any possessive teenage girl and I struggled to set it into the life that I imagined for her, of pension days, coupons and white hair rinses. Yet, as the story unfolded, I saw her become a woman in love as chaste as a June bride. She had met her Kuwaiti prince in the early days of spring, at Larne market. He was alone, grateful for the chatter, she had been willing to talk. Whenever she went to town on a Saturday, they would meet. The smile on her face grew as she told of their teas together and I wondered how they must have looked, his young dark sunny complexion in contrast to the small woman with white hair and weathered pale skin.

One afternoon, jokingly he had asked her to marry him, saying she was his only friend and he would whisk her away back to the Arabian land of Kuwait from miserable, wet Ireland.

I was suddenly jerked to attention – her voice was sincere, to her this was no jest. The love was real. She continued talking, lost in the tale, but her face had changed – a cloud of dark thought had invaded her world.

One Saturday he wasn't at the market, but she continued shopping, she visited the gift shops for some small token of love. Pain grew in her voice as she found words more difficult and her tale began to falter. I watched unable to interrupt as her hands rose in agitation continually forming fists. From what I could piece together, he hadn't noticed her enter the gift shop, engrossed as he talked with a young girlfriend.

Blind with hurt and jealousy she marched between them. Raising her voice, she began to attack him for talking to another girl. Firstly shocked, he tried to talk her down, but she wouldn't let him speak, shouting him down with his own words. So, calmly he turned his back to her and guided the young girl from the shop, then he returned to her side and in a low, stinging voice asked how she dare embarrass him in front of his friends. Then turning abruptly, he left her abandoned. Her strained voice had dropped into silence, and tears welled up from her broken heart.

"Did you ever see him again?" I asked.

"Yes, many times, but he would just ignore

me, crossing the street or taking off into the crowd." She reached her hand towards my face. "You look a lot like him."

I knew that my own dark short hair and brown skin had heightened her pain. We hadn't walked far when she asked me if she had been wrong. I was no longer to be the listener to the tale, I was being asked to participate, to offer some small token of comfort. Looking at her face and listening to her voice, I hesitated before telling her that I felt she had acted hastily in the shop, but he should have given her a chance to say sorry.

"Yes. Yes, he should have let me apologise. If he would let me say sorry, we could have a chance together."

She wanted so much to believe that there was hope. I became overwhelmed as I thought of lost friendships, plans and loves so deep and endlessly passionate.

"You hurt, too."

As the feeling of loss flooded through my body the tears flowing faster, I nodded yes. Then almost naturally, we fell into each other's arms as the tears came. We shared the moment relying on each other for comfort, but there I lost her. Unable to deal with the pain she had brooded on for so long, she searched desperately for reassurance that her prince had not left her forever, that one day he would return. With a pleading look, she turned to me and asked, "When will he come back?"

For many years, I deliberated over my answer. Should I have told her he wouldn't be back? I thought I could help; I told her that he would return in the spring like the time she had first met him. I felt that I had given her a dream for a moment. A look of joy and hope came to light her face, this was all she had hoped for, a chance meeting to plan for.

The old spinster turned to me a final time and reaching out to touch my short dark hair she said, "I know he will come, because you are his messenger and you will ride off into the sky."

She pointed towards the horizon where a lone sunbeam played across the grey sea. Without an answer, she said goodbye and rounded the bend into town again.

Looking back, I query many things about this meeting. Did I create more mischief in her mind by giving her hope?

Most of all, I wonder if I had been a messenger for her, or she for me. For standing alone on the strand, I felt the heavy weight of being the loneliest person in the world and I knew then, as I turned around, I was starting the long journey back to John and love.

# Dotty

by Anthony Curtis

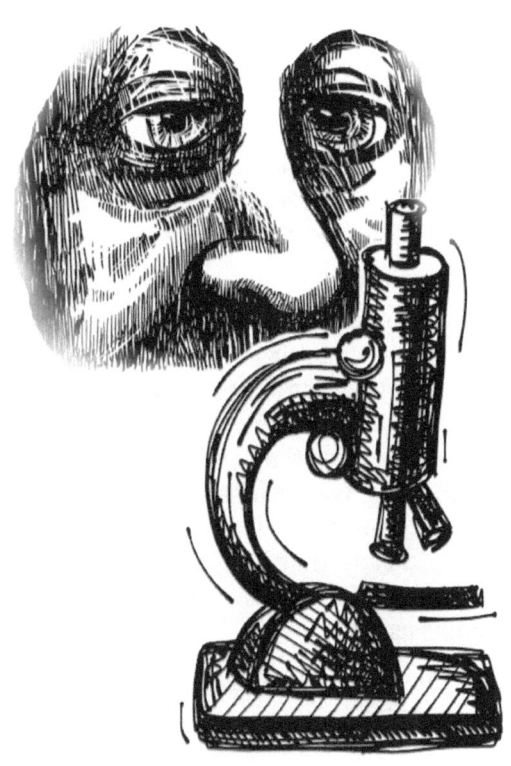

# Dotty

Back in the 1950s, in a world before computers dominated people's lives, Professor Dunk was a lecturer in mathematics at a lesser-known university. He was known to his students as 'The Sparrow' due to his habit of cocking his head to one side when reading.

But Professor Dunk was more than just a mathematician. He secretly experimented with all kinds of things. One day he conducted an almost successful teleportation experiment. The theory, however, proved to be somewhat weaker than the practice, and his television set was teleported into another dimension, an event which caused the professor to decide that his findings should remain secret. After all, the world has enough problems as it is.

The professor was tempted to destroy the formula, but a page full of scribbled mathematical equations was, to him, equal to a Dürer or a Picasso. The formula was fifteen pages long, and as he was unable to store such a quantity of equations in his head, he gave them to a colleague, who promised to reduce them to microdots. He almost scratched his brains out trying of think of a suitable hiding place for the dots. Eventually he found one and was confident that no one would ever find them. He purchased a powerful microscope, and in the evenings he would take the microdots from their hiding place, put them under the apparatus, and sit gazing into it. The image was slightly distorted, but that didn't bother him.

The theory he had published in the science journal 'New Inventions', however, attracted not only scientists, but also military experts, government departments and foreign spies, all of whom had the same goal: to get the formula at all costs.

Too eccentric to marry, Professor Dunk lived alone. He was never lonely though, for his interest in his studies transcended normality. Consequently, he was highly surprised when strangers began to show marked interest in him. Then came the alarming telephone calls. How could anyone dare to threaten the life of a little professor in a lesser-known university? People were after his formula!

Up to this time, no one had given the possibility of microdots a thought, for the professor didn't look like the microdot sort. However, the colleague who had shrunk the formula to almost nothing blabbed his heart out one evening to a platinum blonde who worked for the Defence Department. After ten glasses of whisky, he told her all about the microdots, but he had no idea where they were hidden.

Successfully enticing the professor out of his rooms with a seven-day free holiday in the Hebrides (it was the summer and everyone else was away), the Defence Department proceeded to examine every full stop, comma and dot in every book in the professor's rooms. After five days of intensive searching (nobody could hide something that well), they came to the conclusion that the professor has concocted a hoax and was on an ego trip. They were about to leave when one searcher happened to notice a microscope in the corner of the professor's room. Now what would a little professor of mathematics in a lesser-known university want with a large and expensive microscope? "Of course! Microdots have to be enlarged." The dots did exist.

"We'll find 'em," promised the Defence Minister, thankful that he didn't have to look.

"Ve vill get dem," asserted the foreign spies, "even if ve haff to blow ze old egg-head sky high."

"We'll brainwash him," said the CIA when Dunk had returned from the Hebrides, and they proceeded to do so.

"Where have you hidden the microdots?" demanded an exhausted interrogator.

"I'm wearing them," said the professor, lying spread-eagled on a bed.

"Where?" shouted the interrogator.

"Where? ... Yes...wearing them," said the professor.

"Oh nuts. He isn't wearing a stitch. Shall we liquidate him?" asked the interrogator.

"Our methods may be devious," said the boss, "but we are not in the habit of liquidating little professors from lesser-known universities. Personally, I think he's just plain dotty. Take him home and put him to bed."

The microdots were never found.

Professor Dunk should have lived to a ripe old age, but in the middle of a new, 'improved' experiment, he managed to teleport himself into another dimension and was never seen again.

Where then, had the microdots been hidden?

The riddle was eventually solved by a cub reporter who had followed the professor like a relentless bloodhound. He was aware that the professor's students had nicknamed him 'the Sparrow' because of his head cocking habit, and he was also aware of the existence of the microscope. With a flash of genius, he managed to persuade the professor's lawyers to show him a copy of the will, the ultimate phrase of which helped to satisfy his curiosity:

"... that upon my death I be cremated, wearing my contact lenses."

# The Reunion

by Sharon Westmaas

# The Reunion

She'd surely forgotten me. After all, she hadn't seen me for thirty-five years. I was a child of ten back then and hundreds of children had since passed by. She must be over eighty now, a doddering old thing with her memory gone. But I hadn't forgotten her. So since I was in London, I picked up the phone, dialled her number, and told her who I was.

"What! No! You're here in London? Dear, I've been asking EVERYONE if they have your address. I wanted to invite you to our 60th Anniversary Reunion! You MUST come!"

No, she hadn't forgotten me. Mrs Hunter never forgets her children, and none of her children forget her. We're scattered all over the world now, but Saint Margaret's School made us members of a big happy family with her at the unifying centre.

I distinctly remember my first day, when Mummy and Daddy took me along for the interview. Mrs Hunter smiled at three-year-old me.

"You're the Three Bears, and here are the Three Chairs for you: a big chair for Daddy bear, a medium-sized chair for Mummy bear and a tiny little chair for Baby bear!"

This is a nice place, I thought, and all my fears fled.

Mrs Hunter held her school in the bottom storey of her big wooden house in Camp Street, Georgetown, British Guiana. Camp Street was a wide leafy avenue, its two lanes of traffic separated by a footpath down the middle. Huge flamboyant trees lined the walkway, sometimes covered over in brilliant red blossoms, so that I walked down a red carpet of flowers, feeling very happy and proud in my green-and-white checked uniform.

Mrs Hunter had started her school from scratch with just a handful of boys and girls. On the very next day, one of the girls brought her best friend along "because it's much nicer here," and in that vein, Saint Margaret's continued to grow over the years. It became the most sought-after primary school in the country, where even the Prime Minister sent his children – along with their bodyguards. Learning there was a process of unfolding. There was no specific time when we were told, "OK, the fun's over, now life gets serious." I started at age three and left at age ten, and along the way I learned the three R's and a lot more besides. Learning was an integral part of living, and our own natural eagerness to learn was the driving force. We played, sang, danced, acted, listened to stories, and all the time Mrs Hunter knew each child's strengths and weaknesses. Her aim was to bring out the very best in us. Her formula for excellence was simple, but it worked.

"I wanted a happy school," she told me later, "because only a happy child can learn."

Stress was unheard of, despite long hours and high standards. At midday, most of us went home for lunch and returned for afternoon school, after which there was, naturally, homework. By the time I was six, I was writing my own letters to my mother, who was living in Trinidad at the time. In my final year, I took the entrance exams for a school in England, passed easily and left Saint Margaret's for good.

I never realised how lucky I had been until it was time for my own son to start school in Germany. A tidal wave of dire warnings and grim prophecies washed over me, which I refused to believe. For me, primary school could not be anything else but a place of wonder and joy. I was very wrong.

When I sought out Mrs Hunter a couple of years ago, she was living in a tiny, cramped flat in South London. Guyana had become independent, and Saint Margaret's had been nationalised and turned into a government school. Mrs Hunter had been given the choice of staying on as an employee at her own be-loved school, or retiring. She chose retire-ment, receiving a pension of about three pounds sterling a month. Luckily, she was also eligible for a small British pension.

I found a woman old in years but truly young at heart, brimming over with zest, with a mind as alert and a humour as awake as ever. Of course, she had not for-gotten me. And of course, I went to the Sixty-Years Reunion. So did Marjory who had been my best friend. We screeched when we saw each other in our grown-up versions, and the reminiscing began.

"I was so absolutely thick," Marjory confid-ed, "Kippy and I used to be rivals for bottom of the class. But Mrs Hunter always encour-aged us."

Marjory is now a very gifted and successful

artist.

The room was packed – lots of familiar faces, and lots more unfamiliar ones, all ex-pupils of Mrs Hunter who had ended up in England. There were speeches, tears, laughter, stories, memories, songs, poems, toasts to Mrs Hunter and champagne. And belated thanks. For we all knew now how fortunate we were to have passed though Saint Margaret's.

And fortunate too, that on this one day, so many years later, we could relive the good times and feel the intervening years melt away under a teacher's understanding smile.

# A Busker on Bow Street

by Bob Oliver

## A Busker on Bow Street

I awoke one spring morning in a cold sweat. Something was gnawing at the back of my mind but just for the moment, I couldn't think what it was. Then it hit me in a stomach-wrenching sort of way, just as I was about to take a bite out of my toast and marmalade. I lost all appetite for my breakfast, but did manage a few gulps of my tea, spilling quite a bit over the tablecloth in the process. The reason for this state of mind was that I suddenly remembered that I was due to appear at Bow Street Magistrates' Court at ten thirty, charged with soliciting for alms by playing a musical instrument at Green Park underground station on such and such a date and I'd clean forgotten about this unwelcome appointment.

A quick look in my wallet revealed the state of my financial affairs. It wasn't a pretty picture. I had just enough for my Tube fare to the famous establishment. Glancing at my watch, I had about enough time to go down the Tube and hopefully busk up the money I would need to pay my fine for busking. Grabbing my guitar, tambourine, mouth organ, kazoo and other bits and pieces, I rushed off to West Kensington Tube station and purchased a ticket with nearly all the money I had left in the world. The last thing I wanted was to be caught without a valid ticket and add further to my woes. Anyway, I jumped onto the District Line and, after changing at Earls Court for the Northern Line, headed towards my destination, Green Park.

I was in luck for a change as there wasn't another busker in sight, but this could also mean the transport cops were about. Still, in for a penny, in for a pound. Choosing my site very carefully, next to the poster warning that busking was not allowed and that the maximum fine was twenty-five pounds, I set up my pitch. I must admit I was rather nervous, but I had to make up the money for the fine.

Everything went well. No police turned up, although I heard later they had been on the prowl earlier that morning. The money came in at a steady flow, music to my ears. One tall and distinguished gentleman stopped to listen for quite some time, complimented me on my music and re-quested 'Where do you go to my lovely' (not me – the song). We had a little chat and he threw fifty pence in my guitar case and carried on his way. By now I'd enough money for my fine, so I gathered my things together and headed reluctantly towards my fate.

I arrived at Bow Street Court with time to spare and sat on a hard, wooden bench with my guitar and things, waiting to be called. This was the calm before the storm and my mind began to wander. I imagined all sorts of things like ending up working on a rock pile or worse. Which was silly really as it was only a bye-law I'd broken. At last, my name was called, putting an end to my thoughts.

I stood in the dock alone and awaited the entrance of the magistrate, along with the rest of the court. When he entered, you could have knocked me down with a feather. It was the same tall gentleman who'd paid me a compliment along with fifty pence. I had no choice now but to plead guilty. I waited for the penalty with bated breath as the gentleman, a real gentleman, gave his verdict.

With an evil glint in his eyes and a deep resonant bass voice he said, "Mr. Oliver, shall we say fifty pence?"

I left the court a very happy young man and with enough money in my pocket to purchase my next ticket to adventure, busking on the Tube.

# A Scarecrow in Winter

by Anthony Curtis

## A Scarecrow in Winter

Mist swirled lightly in the woods, stirred by a cold breeze between the trees. Through the mist a man appeared. A woollen balaclava covered most of his head and face. Only his eyes were visible; eyes which stared directly ahead, showing no apparent interest in their surroundings. His arms hung down to his sides, only now and then did he use them to push aside branches, He wore a thick overcoat, which reached almost down to his ankles, and on his feet were sturdy leather boots.

Making his way slowly through the woods, he eventually came to a large clearing. The mist did not allow him to see how large it was, but from the furrows on which he now stood, he judged it to be a ploughed field. He walked along its perimeter and suddenly stopped. Through the mist a vague shadow could be seen. The man thought at first that it was a tree, but decided that it was too symmetrical, it looked rather like a cross. Intrigued, he trod carefully over the muddy, uneven ground towards it. As he came nearer, he recognised the object and laughed out loud.

With a bow and a mock flourish of the hand he said, "Why good morning, Mr Scarecrow, fancy meeting you here!"

The man surveyed the scarecrow with a critical eye. His head was a large pumpkin with slits for eyes and mouth, adorned with an old hat and impaled on a vertical wooden cross. A tattered shirt and dungarees filled with straw concealed the scarecrow's skeletal figure. Straw protruded from the extremities of the slats where his hands and feet should have been. The man plucked nervously at a piece of straw which stuck out of the shirt, then jumped back in alarm as a tiny field mouse appeared from one of the pockets of the dungarees. For a nanosecond in eternity, man and mouse stared at each other; then the mouse sprang to the ground and scurried away.

"Well!" exclaimed the man. "That was most unexpected. Have you got any more surprises for me?"

He shook the post gently, but there was no further activity.

There followed a short silence, then the man said, "You're probably wondering what I'm doing here. Well, I'll tell you. I came here to get away from it all."

He stood staring at his gloves, as if giving the scarecrow time to digest this information.

"You don't believe me," he stated at length. "Well, I'm here, and I'll wager that I'm the only person crazy enough to traverse the woods at such an early hour. It's cold and it's damp, and I don't suppose anyone would care if I caught pneumonia or something, but I should worry."

He flung out his arms. A gesture of despair.

"She left me, you know. And my kids were sent off to New Zealand to their grandparents. Hers, not mine. That's what hurts most. They took her side. Said I never had time for the family - always working. But I ask you, Mr Scarecrow, what else could I do? They couldn't appreciate that it was all for them. A house in the country with all the latest gadgets, everything for their comfort. An ultra-modern dwelling, with solar power to boot.

"If you could walk, Mr Scarecrow, I'd take you there. It's not very far from here. Oh, how the roof sparkles in the sunlight. There's nothing like it for miles around, and the neighbours look at it with envy. But now it's empty, even when I'm there. What's the use of having a large house if there's only one person to live in it? Might as well take a bedsitter. Yes, that's what I'll do. Sell the house. Don't you worry. I'm not too old to start afresh somewhere else."

The harsh cry of a crow interrupted the man who automatically looked upwards, but the mist hung heavily over the field, and he could only see the scarecrow and the soil beneath his feet.

"You know something, Mr Scarecrow? I like you. I can talk to you without the fear of being argued with. It's time someone heard my point of view. Oh, I can't say that I'm always right, but then again, I can't always be wrong, can I? You understand me, don't you?"

The scarecrow made no reply.

The man suddenly grasped the post on which it hung and shook it violently.

Faint rustlings of falling straw.

"Oh, what's the use," growled the man. "You're only a scarecrow, what would you know about anything?"

Then he turned his back on the dilapidated figure, walked towards the woods, and disappeared in the mist.

After a while, the silence he left behind was broken by a flapping of invisible wings, but the unrelenting scarecrow stood with its head hanging down on its chest, apparently not giving a damn about anything.

# Ghostly Laughter

by Shelly Bowers

## Ghostly Laughter

Come and sit yourself down here. You're after stories of fairies, are ye? Now, why would you be after stories of fairies, then? Ah! A thesis no less. One of those college types, are ye?

Ye've come to the right God-forsaken hole to hear of fairies. Every man and woman in this pub has a tale to tell of those beautiful dangerous people and what's more, they'll be fallin' over each other to tell it to ye. But you take it easy; it's a flippant type that talks easily of the fairy folk.

Have I met them, eh? Well, that's a question, Would you believe me if I had? Oh, so you don't believe. Well, why should I tell you if you don't believe? Better than that, why would you want to know if you don't believe?

A sociological study, you say? But what would I know of that? Then again, what would I know of what I saw. Let's say I don't know if I've ever seen fairies, but I've seen something that I don't think many have seen.

Well, I know if you want to hear of that I think that I'd better wet my throat. Mine's a Guinness and a Paddy's; I know a lot of lasses are on the Bailey's now, but that sweet stuff ain't for me. Talking's thirsty work, if you know what I mean.

May God bless you for the drink. Now, let's go and sit by the fire. That's it, make yourself comfy by the last blessed turf fire in Ireland and I'll tell of my fairy folk.

I was born in 1950, yes it seems a lifetime ago. My parents had lived through the war and scenes of the Belfast Blitz were seared into their memories. They had seen hundreds blown to kingdom come and for that very reason every Sunday during the fine summer weather we became pilgrims to the war memorial to remember the men who gave life and freedom to Ireland, Britain, Europe and the world with their souls, their bodies and their youth.

Anyway, Sunday when I was a child was Memorial Day. We gave thanks for our lives and our families, but I was there for the sun, the grass and the roses, twirling with my hands in the air and as my dress lifted, I would find myself rising into the sky above the great oaks.

In circles I would spin, higher and higher until I could reach the clouds and touch their cotton wool with my fingertips. Then fall to the earth and lie on the green, with rose petals for a pillow and the sky revolving over my head. It was then that they would come to play, those beautiful girls. They were older, but they called me by my name. Mary, come and play. Mary, come and dance. I raised my head from the grass and saw they were beautiful and wore dresses of fresh poppies. They had lips rouged with blood, porcelain white skin and long dark tresses as black as funeral ribbon.

They danced, skipped and laughed, giggled, laughed and sang, laughed and danced. They would take me by my tiny hands and we would play ring-a-ring-a- roses, as their dark long curls flew in the breeze and the sun grew warm in the sky. Their faces, those of loved ones, cousins, sisters, daughters never known, but near, unborn but alive. My tiny hands in the sisters', I would dance and remember the pain and fear, the hurt and the death of war, but more than that, we danced and laughed for life: the life of the lost men.

We would dance round the obelisk and chant the names of the soldiers and with each name, the life of love, laughter and happiness would flow. This was the lost feelings of a lifetime cut short, a lost ghost.

I would dance in fear, but the sisters would smooth my dark curly hair and laugh, lift me high in the air and sing soothingly of lost love and children unknown to me. They would weave daisies in my hair and hang garlands of poppies around my soft white neck, hug and love me as a lost child, throw rose petals at my feet and spread their arms wide for my hugs when my chubby little arms spread forth for acceptance, to embrace the love unfulfilled.

Then the shadow would come, the sun would die and my Granda would come to lift me into his huge shipbuilder's arms and say "Enough". The sisters cringed in his sight, clinging to the obelisk as he raised his staff of hawthorn. All would flee before his wrath.

My sisters would fly leaving only the sad wreaths of death, paper poppies crumbling dry in the wind, leaving me alone in the evening light – alone under the shadow of the obelisk, without the love, without the song, without the dance, with only the echo of ghostly laughter.

I am the child the fairies didn't steal.

# Flitzo

by Anthony Curtis

# Flitzo

Jenny handed the letter to her husband.

"Here, Jim, read the last paragraph," she said, knowing how much he hated letters from Aunt Emma.

"... and now for the exciting part.

I know you'll never believe me (nobody ever does), but there seems to be a plague of bluebottles in our house. With the weather we're having at the moment, they must be reproducing like rabbits. We've sprayed them with that special spray which is not supposed to upset the balance of nature. You know, Jenny. Flitzo. It's supposed to be the best thing there is. It gets rid of flies, mosquitos, bugs and cockroaches, with no risk of poisoning ourselves. But no matter how often we spray, for every fly we get rid of, it seems that two take its place.

And that's not all. I'm certain that the creatures are learning to hide. Fred goes along with this. He's always remarked on how dumb bluebottles are, but he's not so certain now. They normally just sit there and let themselves be pulverised ..."

He read on ...

"... they seem to hide in every nook and cranny. We've installed mosquito nets on all our windows, but they still keep on coming. I shudder to think how many maggots are crawling about in the wainscoting. We went to the Sanitary Department last week, but they were on strike, and still are. Fred says the flies have probably built up a resistance to Flitzo. I do hope not. It's terribly expensive."

There followed the usual greetings to the family and "... why don't you visit us anymore? Love, Aunt Emma."

Jim handed the letter back to his wife. "Overdoing it a bit, isn't she?"

"I suppose you're right," said Jenny. "I don't think I can really accept her suggestion that flies are getting clever enough to conceal themselves."

Jim pondered for a while and then said, "Yes, it does sound improbable, doesn't it? But if it were true, and I'm not saying for one moment that it is, it wouldn't be very good for us, would it?"

Jim laughed nervously.

"What are you talking about, Jim?"

"I once heard a professor on the radio say that if insects ever achieve intelligence, our intelligence that is, the human race will probably vanish within a week.

And the irony of it all is, the world itself would be saved from further pollution. He also said something about there being no final stage of evolution. That all our meddling with genetic engineering and cloning will eventually change the natural order of things. There'll be new evolutionary stages, and heaven knows what will happen then."

Jenny shuddered. "You're making me nervous, Jim. And all because of a stupid letter."

Jim laughed. "I was only kidding, darling. Let's forget it. Aunt Emma's obviously trying to draw attention to herself."

They promptly forgot the matter and played cards for the rest of the evening.

Having given the television the night off, they failed to learn that thousands of wasps had been terrorising the population in the southern counties.

That night, although Jim slept soundly, Jenny, more influenced by Aunt Emma's letter than she would have liked to admit, kept her eyes open for bluebottles. But, of course, there weren't any, and eventually, she, too, drifted off to sleep.

She was awakened in the wee small hours by a buzzing sound. She switched on the light and surveyed the walls and the ceiling. Nothing. She was about to switch off the light when it occurred to her that she had not looked behind the bed, which was not completely against the wall. She did so. Six extremely large mosquitos clung to the wall as if they were waiting for something.

Shocked, Jenny softly opened and closed the bedroom door, and went down to the kitchen.

The Flitzo was in the cupboard under the sink, which seemed to be infested with wood-lice.

Back in the bedroom, she sprayed the mosquitos. They fell onto the carpet. Placing the spray can on the dressing table, Jenny got into bed again.

An hour later, she was awakened by a buzzing sound. She turned the light on and surveyed the walls and the ceiling. No mosquitos. She looked behind the bed. Nothing on the wall or on the carpet. She began to scratch her neck. It was itching terribly, and in more places than one. Jim slept soundlessly on.

In panic, she searched and searched. No mosquitos. Anywhere.

By now, her neck was considerably swollen, and Jenny was beginning to feel drowsy. She lay on the bed. Very soon she slipped into a coma ...

From a small air grille behind the dressing table, a dozen mosquitos appeared and zoomed towards the bed.

"Here is enough blood for a million offspring," thought one.

"Thanks to Flitzo," thought another.

And without opening their long mouths, the rest of the mosquitos agreed.

# That's Cricket!

by Dorothy Elchlepp

## That's Cricket!

The sun seems to shine a bit brighter somehow when it beams on a village cricket match. The broad green glistens like emerald against the shade of encircling trees, and the cricketers move through their ritual clad in dazzling white.

All this came back to me one nostalgic September, no, not in England but in a small town in southern Germany, only a few miles from Freiburg. Denzlingen had been twinned with North Hykeham in Lincolnshire for ten years. A team consisting of young expat Englishmen, Australians, Irishmen, Scots and two Sri Lankans had formed a cricket club and offered to play a match against a team consisting of players only from Sri Lanka.

The German spectators, eager to know more about our national game, were to be given a commentary over a loudspeaker. One couldn't expect a pitch in the middle of a football field to live up to any of our village greens, and a piece of matting had been laid down between the wickets. I soon realised that the public were getting impatient.

As a girl, I had watched the game so often. My brother played for Sussex in the fifties, and I had often accompanied my father to Lords or the Oval for a Test Match. Two nephews played for Eastbourne College. In other words, I knew the rules.

Back to Denzlingen. All eyes were riveted on the centre of the green where a young man abruptly leapt forward in giant strides, swung a stiff arm and hurled a small red ball at blistering speed towards a target formed by three upright sticks (the stumps) joined at the top by two bails.

My immediate neighbours in the recreation ground stand started to put questions to me, so I explained that the man guarding the wicket was the batsman who meets the missile with his bat and a thwack sends the ball towards one of the crouching fielders. He snaps it up barehanded and the batsman decides it's not safe to run. This is cricket; he doesn't have to.

My neighbours started to show interest. I continued and gradually the picture emerged. Two wickets set 22 yards apart, each defended by a batsman, two bowlers attacking the wickets, one bowls an over of six balls, then fields while his mate bowls from the other end of the pitch. This bowler tries with either a fast or a slow spinning delivery to bounce the ball past the batsman and demolish the wicket. If a batsman tries to block or swipe the ball and it strikes him instead of his bat, the umpire rules 'leg before wicket' and he's OUT! If he knocks a ball over the boundary, he gets a six. If a flying ball is caught, the batsman is OUT. When ten of a team's eleven men are out, the 'innings' ends and the other side comes in to bat.

Well, I thought, that's enough for a start and I felt I had stirred up some interest. However, I feel that cricket will never catch on in Germany; they simply get too impatient with slow play.

Cricket, traditionally England's national game, has a longer history than most team games and its basic rules have scarcely altered since the 1700's and the game was old then. Royal household accounts show that Prince Edward, later Edward II, played it at Westminster in 1300.

Cricket has provided one expression that is now heard in many connections, that is 'hat trick', which dates back to the days when cricketers wore top hats. Any player who took three wickets with three successive balls was presented with a white top hat.

The old game still stirs English hearts. Newspaper headlines proclaim the loss of a Test Match with words that frighten foreign investors: "ENGLAND TOPPLES", one recently screamed in large capitals.

On that day in Denzlingen, as a thwack of willow was met by a mild ripple of applause, I couldn't help thinking that here, on the edge of the Black Forest, was a little piece of England.

⤜⤛

# Annie

by Anthony Curtis

## Annie

"Grandma!" called Annie softly.

There was no reply, so little Annie tip-toed to the house to tell Mummy all about Grandma, who had chosen a very funny place to go to sleep.

She had expected some sort of reaction to her story, but she was totally unprepared for the commotion that followed. Mummy dropped a baking tray onto the floor, which made a terrible noise. Then, with a "Stay right where you are!" she rushed out into the garden, and little Annie, afraid that she had done something wrong, sat on a stool and pouted.

On the kitchen table stood a large plate of freshly baked currant buns. They smelled delicious. She only had to reach her hand out – but no, maybe she'd said something wrong – if she took one now, Mummy might be angry.

Three long minutes later, Mummy came

into the kitchen and disappeared into the front room. Annie heard her voice, very loud and agitated.

"Yes, Doctor, I think it's her heart. My husband's at work and I'm not sure what to do."

The receiver was replaced, and Mummy came back into the kitchen.

"Mummy," began Annie, wanting to ask about Grandma, but her mother said, "Don't bother me just now, Annie. You can have a bun if you want, but stay here and be quiet."

Annie slid off the stool and surveyed the buns. She wasn't sure which one to take so she recited, "Eeny, meeny, miny" pointing to each one in turn. Finally stopping at "moe", she decided that this particular bun was too small, so she looked for the one that had the most currants.

She was about to take the bun, but was interrupted by a wailing sound that came from the street. She knew what it was, of course. She'd seen one on the telly. It was an ambulance. The wailing was so loud Annie put her hands over her ears. When she removed them, the wailing had stopped. There was a slamming of doors. Annie grasped the kitchen stool and dragged it to the window. Wobbling precariously, she pulled back the lace curtains so that she had a clear view of the front garden. Yes, there was the ambulance, standing at the kerb opposite the front gate. A big red cross was painted on its side. Two large men in white were unloading something. It looked like a bed on wheels, and they pushed it over the front lawn (What will Mummy say?) and were soon out of sight. Annie clambered down from the stool and ran to the kitchen door. She could see her mother and the two men standing by the roses. Then the men lifted Grandma and put her on the bed on wheels. She was still asleep! Then they wheeled her away.

Annie didn't want to climb onto the stool again, it was too tiring, so she turned her attention once more to the buns. This time she took the first one that came. Munching loudly, she heard once more the slamming of doors, but the ambulance didn't wail when it drove off.

She was licking her fingers and contemplating the next bun when Mummy came into the kitchen, followed by the doctor. Mummy's eyes were red from weeping and the doctor looked very serious.

"I'll make a cup of tea," she said to the doctor.

"Thanks, but no," said the doctor." I'll be wanted elsewhere, most likely."

He came over to Annie and patted her gently on the head, but he didn't put his hand in his pocket for sweets as he usually did, so Annie climbed back on the stool and began to pout again. The doctor said goodbye, Mummy saw him out and then, as she came back and put the kettle on, Annie asked, "Mummy? Where's Grandma gone?"

She came to her daughter and pressed her to her bosom.

"Oh, my darling, Grandma's gone away. We'll never see her again."

"Never?"

With tears running down her cheeks, Mummy shook her head, and not knowing quite why, Annie felt like crying, too. Breaking from Mummy's embrace, she ran into the garden to the place where Grandma had lain. She saw the broken roses and suddenly she understood everything.

Grandma had gone to the same place where Joey had gone. Only a week ago,

Joey had fallen off his perch and had lain quite still at the bottom of his cage. Mummy had taken him away, and in answer to Annie's questions had said that Joey had gone to heaven. Annie wasn't quite sure where heaven was, but it must be a very nice place. The next day, Mummy had come home with another Joey.

Fingering the roses, Annie thought, "If Grandma's gone to heaven, Mummy will bring me another one, but this time I shan't creep up behind her and say 'Booooooo!'"

# Lost Dreams

by Deirdre Mclaughlin

## Lost Dreams

The sky over Winchester was overcast and the first drops of rain landed on her shoulders as she pressed her palm against the brass push plate on the door of the Red Lion.

She hadn't been in for ages. It may seem weird to long for the musty, beery tang that often hangs in the air of a public house, but this had been 'her' pub. She loved to be among friends, to chat about people, business, politics or just ordinary everyday life. She had found lots of friends there, people she would talk to once or twice and who then vanished for a couple of months only to return with renewed energy, more experience, new ideas. She, on the other hand, seemed to derive all her strength, her energy and experience from this place and its people. She used to love just sitting and listening to folk talking about their interests and their way of life. She saw this as her path to wisdom. People were always very kind, taking her into their confidence, buying her drinks or just passing the time of day. She knew nearly everyone, either by sight or as an acquaintance. She had her friends among the bartenders, the staff and the regulars. In short, it was her dream come true being a part of this big 'family'.

She spent a lot of time just hanging out in this special place and it was little wonder that her other interests suffered as a result. So much so that she had to give herself a break. So, one evening in late summer, she parted from her friends and what had become her second home.

At first, the separation made her feel a bit strange. Then she felt a kind of chill going through all her friendships. Over the next three months, things didn't turn out as well as she had hoped; people didn't call her as much as they had promised, and she got the feeling that something was going wrong, something had changed. She longed to go back; She suffered horribly under the strain of being away.

This grey November evening was her first oppor- tunity to return. She went down to the pub at her old time, at about six in the evening. She had arranged to meet one of her girlfriends at half past six. She saw the change immediately: the green-painted door, once well-polished and spotless, was dirty, with the paint peeling off. At the bottom of the stairs there was a swing door with a window in the upper half – one of those covered with colourful flowers and ornaments. She was shocked: the door was sagging on its hinges and the window was so grimy that she could hardly see inside. Suddenly she stopped. What on earth was wrong? She listened hard: Nothing! Where were all the happy voices she used to hear when she came down the steps, the soft murmuring and clattering that drifted up the stairs to the street? Now all was silent: no voices, no chinking of glasses, only a faint humming of a far-away singer emanating from the speakers of a sound system.

She looked through the window into a gloomy room, empty, unfamiliar, grey. She was taken aback. What had happened? Was it because it had turned to winter, or had things really changed in such a short time? She walked in; no voices greeted her. She looked around: The bar, once so famil-iar, bright, crowded and vibrant, was now dirty, nearly deserted. The tables and chairs, once so neatly arranged, now stood around in complete disorder.

A voice asked her what she would like to drink. She ordered her usual tipple from a totally unfamiliar barman and sat down to wait.

The ringing of a phone in the distance broke the silence. The barman hurried excitedly towards the sound as if it might save him from dying of boredom. As he stood with his eyes turned towards the entrance, she could see his face clearly. It brightened up when he put the receiver to his ear, as if he were used to changing his expression when talking to a customer. But that look vanished quickly as he told the caller to wait a second. He called out her name. Surprised, she left her stool and went over to the phone. It was her friend, who was full of apologies but had to work late and would not be there for another hour or so.

She pulled out her mobile phone: no signal, not even a bar or a blip; that's why the call had come in on the landline. She couldn't even log on to social networks. What was she supposed to do for another hour if no one came in? In despair, she ordered another drink. What now? No one to talk to, nothing interesting going on. In the mirror opposite she could see the stairs and the door. At least she could see who was coming down.

With no conversation and not even a newspaper in sight, her attention turned to offline games. After what seemed like an eternity, she had crashed out on Candy Crush, got totally tired of Tetris and had her fill of Funny Furries when she heard footsteps descending.

A glance in the mirror told her that this was definitely not her friend. So, she snapped the wallet of her phone shut and was on the point of rising to leave when she heard the unmistakable clickety-click of high heels. Long legs appeared in the mirror followed by a miniskirt, an old pullover, an orange scarf, and a laughing face surrounded by a mop of red hair – a face which was more familiar to her than anything else since she had arrived. After a kiss on each cheek, they sat down, ordered drinks and exchanged the latest news and gossip.

She learned what had happened to the Red Lion. The owner had changed and many of the old bar staff and regulars had left. The new owner had soon run out of money. Prices had increased and people had gone where they could get the same but cheaper. Some of her friends still met up there occasionally. But many of them had left; they had got better jobs, moved away, vanished forever. What remained was now a small, unhappy crowd.

She sat there disheartened. How could all this have happened without her knowing? After a while, she decided to go away forever from this place, the place that had once been so dear to her. The dream was gone.

She put the blame on her friends for not telling her. It was worth rethinking the nature of those friendships again. She wasn't sure any more if those people had really been her friends.

A little while later, she and her friend left the Red Lion arm in arm, determined to find another place where they could relax and on her part, fired with a new desire to feel at home – and be part of a big, happy family once again.

# Blacky

by Anthony Curtis

# Blacky

Every village, every town, every city he visited lacked what he was looking for, and his frustration was immense. Until one day he was lucky. How and why (if you're not inclined to cheat) is explained at the end of this story.

He was born in the year 2200 and died eighteen years later. By 2214 he knew exactly what he was going to be. He had visited an antique shop and found an ancient picture book. An old man, (who was himself almost an antique), let him have it for next to nothing, for no-one bought such things any more.

The crucial moment came in 2216, when, pressed to choose a career, he had an argument with his parents.

"That is what I want to be," he said, showing them one of the pictures in the book.

"What?" asked father, and mother swooned on the water bed.

Revived, mother said, "But you can't. They're not needed any more."

"Don't you understand, son?" said father. "They're extinct."

"I don't care. That's what I want to be. Even if it means starvation or worse."

With tears and threats and a final handout, he set off on his quest.

By 2217, he was ready to give up; but then he found what he was looking for; in another antique shop. This time the article was expensive; the dealer said it was the only one left in the world. The accessories he could have for nothing. The searcher willingly gave almost all of his money to the dealer, who shook his head and stared in wonder at the apparition that now stood before him.

This apparition marched jauntily through the streets while jeering inhabitants followed him to the outskirts of the town.

"You don't exist any more," said an old man. "You're extinct," said another.

"You've got bats in the belfry," said a young woman.

He hastened his steps and soon left the people behind him.

He wandered and wandered, for there was still something that he needed; and in April 2218, with a great whoop of joy, he found it.

A tall, thin tower, attached to an ancient ruin. It was the only structure he had ever seen that did not have hundreds of panels to soak up the sun's energy. The tower was about thirty feet high and had steel rungs jutting out of it. He fastened his paraphernalia and began to climb.

When he reached the top, he began to descend the tower from the inside.

On reaching the bottom, he fell asleep from exhaustion, never to wake again.

While he was asleep, an explosion occurred, and the tower he had climbed fell slowly but surely to the ground, like the Tower of Pisa had done a hundred years earlier.

Later, when the dust had settled, a group of men with steel helmets gathered round the thing that had been flung out by the force of the explosion.

"I thought they didn't exist anymore," said one of the men.

"So did I," said another, staring at the body of

a young man dressed as a chimney sweep.

And the youngster's face was as black as a starless night.

Later, a plaque was unveiled on the site of the tragedy:

Here lie the remains
of the last chimney sweep in the
world. He had obviously been born
two hundred years too late; for the
world has been powered by solar
energy for the last hundred and fifty
years.

Let the death of this young man be a
lesson to us all. We must walk boldly
into the Future, and not retreat into
the Past, for that is the way to
destruction.

This plaque was laid by
His Excellency The
World President
Anno Domini 2218.

# The Table

by William David Halbert

# The Table

It's just a table, just an ordinary table. At least in appearance.

It's a simple table, most of a metre high, small grey and white checks on its Formica top, edged with a silver aluminium strip. A simple pedestal table that can be found in coffee shops throughout the country. This particular coffee shop is long closed and the table now stands in a revered corner of my small, dimly lit apartment in this un-fashionable part of town; a light in the darkness of this heart's long night.

It was across this very table that I first saw her. To be sure, she was beautiful. And like the legendary Helen whose face launched a thousand ships, her face pos-sessed a mystic quality setting her apart from all others. When she walked into a room, all eyes turned, both men's and women's. Her most amazing feature was her hair. It was satiny and soft as down in texture, a cascade of dark brown, almost black, silk falling to her lower back. Her hair was only one of many distinctive characteristics and perfectly complemented her long, lithe and soft features. Yet her presence, the sheer strength of being – of the radiant soul within – was the driving attraction of this wonder.

As was my usual habit, I sat down at my usual table in my usual cafe for my usual Earl Grey. Yet as soon as I sat down, I was captivated by her as though the rest of the world simply fell away. She was sitting there with a book in hand and a glass of Talisker on the table, her presence warming the rest of the room. The novel she was fixed on, as surely as I was fixed on her, was Spanish. I would learn later on of her passion for all things Spanish – dress, music, food and in particular, these Spanis gothic novels. There was one exception to this fascination – her love of Scottish single malts, Talisker in particular. That's how it was when I first saw her: her beauty, her Spanish novel, her Talisker. But she had not taken notice of me, nor had she reason to. Instead, after a while, she paid her bill and left.

It was then that I first noticed how the table took on an appearance different from the others. It seemed translucent – as if of its own power, or possibly from some faint remnant of her presence, it began to glow, its surface shining like pearl in the midst of a grey plastic ocean.

How could I but move to it as it called out to me? Putting my hand on the table, I felt the wondrous though strange warmth invading my senses. It was as though the table physically held me to it. I was unable to be free, yet content to be captive.

Sitting there, I was startled as she returned, looking for her key. As if by some kind of magic, I could feel her key in my hand, its smooth and jagged edges pressing into my skin as if put there by some unseen force. Truly, the key had not been there before as I had admired the table's smoothness and emptiness, a perfect metaphor of my own life. Yet in my hand was the key. I gave it to her as she sat down at what was now our table.

In gratitude, she called the waiter and ordered two more Taliskers. I remember nothing of what was said. I see only her beautiful hair shining, eyes flashing, skin glowing. If only I could reach out and become part of this scene once more... Whenever we went out it was always to that cafe, and always to that table, our table. Oh, what that table saw and heard! It witnessed our happiness, our sorrows and even my nervous hand's fumbling when I proffered the ring for her eternal hand. So many times we returned, even after we had in delight exchanged our vows for a lifetime together.

I shall not tell the details of her tragic, sudden and untimely death as in the telling the pain of her passing comes back to life. Only know that the wind swept her away from me, leaving me lost and alone. It was not until years later, when I heard of the cafe's demise that I set eyes again on our table.

# THE TASTE OF RAIN

The door was ajar on the condemned building, slated for the wrecking ball, when I entered. Years of misuse followed by years of disuse had claimed their toll on the cafe. Scattered rocks lay on the floor next to shards of glass their throwers had broken.

Dust was everywhere and a certain damp mustiness emanating from the rotting beams lingered in the air, stifling my breath, suffocating all sound. The few chairs and tables that remained were broken and scattered around. Only the bar at the end of the room was intact, though thickly covered with a layer of grime.

Then I spied a very singular, dim glow emanating from a point just out of sight behind the bar. As I approached, the familiar, warm and eerie glow grew greater with every step. Once again, the table called out to me. When it had done so before it had, for a time, saved my life. Only now I was able to return the favour. I left the café, knowing I would never set foot in it again.

Through my tears I could see my true love's face as if again we met for the very first time.

# Land of the Dragons

by Arja Faller-Nenonen

## Land of the Dragons

Mum told us about trolls and giants, but they lived in a very faraway land. They were fairy tales. What she did not know about, but we did, were dragons. In Wales they came in all sizes. Some were so small you could not see them. How small can you get before you disappear? Some dragons were so large you could not see them. They filled the universe. We were just fleas in their scales. Then there were the normal-sized dragons, of course. They were clear to see. Take Caerphilly Mountain. That's a medium-sized dragon sleeping peacefully. It was great fun climbing to the top of its round back on a Sunday morning to look down on the town with its castle and the surrounding countryside. From there you could see the backs of other dragons curled up in their sleep. They were all waiting for a time when knights in armour would come back to give battle. Then they would wake up and fight again.

My brother and I dressed up as knights in shining armour. Mum's discarded winter boots, tunics made of sheets and curtains, cardboard helmets and wooden swords painted silver and turned into chainmail and brilliantly clashing steel. Most of the time we only frightened smaller dragons down in the old quarry at the end of our street. They fell hissing into the pond, cooled down and fell back asleep again.

Many of the valleys had lots of dragons hiding in mineshafts. They were the really mean ones. In Aberfan they even swallowed up children by sending a colliery waste tip slithering into their school. It was all in the news. We watched the devastation on the telly and our teacher told us about those poor children dying. The whole school kept a minute's silence for them.

Inside Caerphilly Castle lived some bigger dragons, too. Some of them were extremely dangerous, because they were not really asleep, only pretending. They had made a ruin of the castle and were now lurking in the corners of the dark towers and passages.

Then one day ... I could see the danger, but nobody listened when Mum suddenly got this craze about the colour midnight blue – the favourite colour of dragons. First, the kitchen cabinets, tables and chairs became midnight blue. Every day after school, we discovered something new, which had turned this colour. It was very worrying.

One day we found that the walls and ceiling of our upstairs loo on the half landing had also turned this terrifying colour of midnight blue. I told them to lock the door and bolt it from the outside. They only laughed. We never entered that loo again, but used the one downstairs which was bright primrose yellow. It was a friendly colour, but the paint was peeling, and we lived in constant fear of that midnight blue paint pot. We lay awake at night worrying about the upstairs loo not being locked shut. In the end, we found a solution. We put marbles in front of the door, so we would hear when something came out and fell over them. We had a good night's sleep at last and heard nothing.

Next morning, Dad gave us a right telling off. He claimed he had nearly broken his neck slipping on the marbles. We tried to tell him it was not our fault. It was the dragon.

The move came in the summer holidays. Mum and Dad explained to us it was because Dad had got a better job in the South of England, but we knew better. It was all because of that wretched dragon in the midnight blue lavatory. But why did we have to move so far, to a place where there are no caves or mineshafts? The seaside has no wild crags or coves, only pebbles. There is not a single dragon in this land.

My brother and I dream about them still.

We will never forget the Land of the Dragons, but we know we can never return.

# The Fear

by Anthony Curtis

## The Fear

Checking a pile of homework, Mrs Leary was interrupted by one of her pupils who had rushed into the classroom.

"Mrs Leary," he cried. "There's a bomb in the playground!"

"What are you prattling about, Timothy? What do you mean, a bomb?"

"There's a bomb in the playground," Timothy repeated.

"If this is one of your silly pranks ... I'll ..."

The teacher walked quickly out of the classroom leaving the threat unfinished, and the boy followed apprehensively.

The children in the playground looked as if they were waiting for a cue from a film director. They stood stock still in a circle staring at a boy who was lying full-length on the ground, his arms folded under his body, as if hugging something.

Mrs Leary advanced, but one of the girls said,

"Don't go near him, Miss. He's sitting on a bomb."

"He's not sitting, he's lying," the teacher said, "but he can't lie there for ever."

She called to the boy. "Peter, get up, there is no sense in what you're doing. You'll not be saving any lives that way."

Peter stood up, slowly, a sickly grin on his face. The bomb now lay at his feet. It was perfectly round and rather uninteresting.

"It's a dud," said one of the children.

"Just wait until it goes off before you say that," retorted Peter.

A few of the others giggled, and Mrs Leary began to suspect a practical joke.

"Now then," she said, her voice stern, "who's responsible for this?"

"No one," said Peter, his voice dripping innocence, "at least not from our school. A man in blue overalls rolled it into the playground and shouted; 'Here's a present for you.' Then he ran off."

"Is this true?"

All the children nodded their heads, and Mrs Leary, who believed emphatically that they would not collectively deceive her, felt a pang of fear.

Suddenly she realised, and it was a bit of a shock, that she had no idea what bombs really looked like. Surely they should have fins, or fuses sticking out of them. This one appeared to be so lifeless.

"All right, children. I want you to leave the playground. All of you. And quietly. Go to the old barn on the other side of Farmer Mulligan's orchard, and leave the apples where they are. In the meantime, I'll telephone the police. Now move."

The children moved. All except Timothy, who lingered behind.

"Well, Timothy, what's wrong? I'd get going if I were you."

The boy hesitated and then said, "If you please, Miss, my father's in the army. He's a bomb disposal expert."

"Oh really! And may I ask what that has to do with the present situation?"

"I thought I could try to defuse the bomb. My father showed me how."

"Young man," said Mrs Leary. "It's clear to me that you are out of your mind. If you don't get out of here right now, you'll get detention. Now move!"

Knowing the teacher could be taken at her word, Timothy moved.

Mrs Leary went to the staff room and telephoned the police. Three minutes later, there were howls of sirens and three police cars skidded into the playground. A dozen officers sprang out of the cars and formed a circle around the offending article. Nonchalantly, as if he had all the time in the world, a plainclothes policeman, who reminded Mrs Leary of her late father, walked over to her.

"Mornin' Ma'am. Bit of a problem, eh? Well, we'd better take a look – but I'd be obliged if you would stand clear. Or better still, leave the area."

"I prefer to stay," said Mrs Leary firmly. The Inspector shrugged, "As you wish."

Then he walked over to the police-ringed bomb and surveyed it. After a minute, he bent over, took the contraption in his hands and shook it. Then, to Mrs Leary's consternation, let it fall to the ground. There was a hollow metallic clang. The bomb bounced once, rolled a few inches, wobbled, and then broke in half.

Her heart beating rapidly, Mrs Leary thought the Inspector was either a very brave man or an idiot.

"Your kids have been having you on, Ma'am," he said. "It's a fake."

Embarrassed, Mrs Leary started to apologise, but the Inspector brushed her words away with a wave of his hand and said, "I'll be off now. You can keep it as a souvenir."

When the police had gone, Mrs Leary picked the pieces up and took them into the class-room.

I'll find out who did this, she thought, savagely, even if I have to punish every single one of them.

It was then that she noticed a small slip of pa-per taped to the inside of one half of the bomb. Pencilled in rough characters were the words:

*You was lucky this time.*

My children don't use grammar like that, she thought, and was proud of the fact. Some-thing was wrong.

And she remembered what she had, up until now, deliberately cast out of her mind. Back in Belfast, all those years ago. A flat bicycle tyre had saved her life.

She had been late and was only a hundred yards away from the school when, with a loud roar, it burst into flames. She was blown to the ground. Seconds later, debris flew over her head, and then the screams started, those of the injured mingling with her own.

Her heart pounding, Mrs Leary stared out of the window to the orchard where the children were playing.

Please let it be a practical joke ... Please!

# Acknowledgements

Some of these stories first appeared in The Written Word, a journal for English-speaking residents of Baden-Württemberg, Germany.

The publishers would like to thank the authors of the original stories for offering their work for publication and similarly to express their gratitude to all who were involved in producing both The Written Word and the present collection, thereby enabling these stories to reach the wider audience they so rightly deserve.